THE UNICORN'S SECRET

#1

Moonsilver

by Kathleen Duey
illustrated by Omar Rayyan

ALADDIN PAPERBACKS

New York   London   Toronto   Sydney   Singapore

For all the day-dreamers.

First Aladdin Paperbacks edition November 2001
Text copyright © 2001 by Kathleen Duey
Illustrations copyright © 2001 by Omar Rayyan

Aladdin Paperbacks
An imprint of Simon & Schuster
Children's Publishing Division
1230 Avenue of the Americas
New York, NY 10020

Designed by Debra Sfetsios
The text of this book was set in Golden Cockerel ITC.
Printed and bound in the United States of America
8 10 9
Library of Congress Control Number: 2001046114
ISBN 0-689-84269-4

✦ CHAPTER ONE

Heart Avamir was tired.

Everyone else had gone home.

It would be dark soon.

The stiff wheat stubble had scraped her hands bloody. There were long scratches on her bare feet.

Heart smiled. Her sack was half full. The harvesters had hurried through the fields this year, missing more grain than usual.

Lord Dunraven wouldn't like the gleaners finding so much fallen grain. But the people of Ash Grove were happy. They would have more bread this winter.

Lord Dunraven didn't need their little bit of gleaned wheat.

He owned every wheat field, every barley field, every hillside.

He owned the forest on the other side of the Blue River. The bridge that crossed the Blue River and the road that led to Derrytown belonged to him, too. Lord Dunraven owned towns and villages.

He owned everything.

Old Simon cleared his throat and spat. "What's that?" he asked, pointing.

Heart faced the sunset. Something was moving at the far end of the field, near the edge of a grove of old oak trees.

"A deer?" she replied.

"Looks like a cow," Simon said.

Heart squinted. "I can't tell." The animal was moving farther into the deep shadows.

"Whose cow would be out for wolves to find?" Simon asked. He tied up their wheat sacks with twine he kept in his pockets.

"I'll go see," Heart said.

Simon nodded. "Hurry back. No playing."

Heart glanced at Simon's angular face and thin gray hair. She wished that he loved her. But she knew he didn't.

Simon Pratt was not her father, after all. Nor was he an uncle or a grandfather or any kind of family.

Five years before, Simon had found her sleeping in the high grass by the Blue River. He had come upon her that morning the way someone stumbles across a nest of quail eggs.

Simon told her all about it. He'd been gathering firewood among the cottonwood trees by the river. She had been wrapped in a beautiful blanket, her hair knotted and tangled.

"Can you see what it is?" Simon shouted now.

Startled from her thoughts, Heart whirled around.

"Not yet!" she shouted over her shoulder. Whatever the animal was, it was deep in the dappled shade now.

Walking slowly toward the edge of the woods,

Heart tried to recall something, anything, from *before* the morning Simon had awakened her in the tall grass.

She couldn't.

She never could.

Her first memory was this:

Her eyes had flown open and her breath had come quicker than a startled rabbit. And Simon had been there, leaning over her, with his sharp-nosed face, his dark eyes and dark clothes.

And that was it.

Heart could remember everything back to that instant, perfectly. But then her memories just *ended*.

Simon had called her "Girl" for weeks. He had not named her. Ruth Oakes had done that. But he had fed her. She was alive. She knew she should be grateful.

But all the other children in Ash Grove knew their parents. They knew their grandparents and their great-grandparents. They didn't trust her. They wouldn't play with her, or even talk to her.

"What is it?" Simon called. "Why can't you see?"

Startled again, Heart stopped, peering into the dusky shade under the oak trees.

"It's a horse!" she called back, surprised. No one in Ash Grove owned horses, except Tin Blackaby. "A mare!"

"Then it's Blackaby's," Simon called. "Leave it alone!"

Heart nodded. She felt sorry for the horse.

Blackaby was Lord Dunraven's steward. He counted out crops and chicks and sheep and corn. He weighed out the peppers and onions people raised to sell to the Derrytown merchants. He told people how much they had to give to Lord Dunraven and how little they could keep. He was not kind. He worked his men and his horses hard.

"Blackaby's men will come," Simon shouted. "They'll think we're trying to steal it."

"Wait," Heart pleaded. "This isn't Tin Blackaby's horse."

"You're sure?" Simon shouted.

"Yes!" Heart called back. She could see the mare better now. It was white. She'd never seen a white horse in Tin Blackaby's corrals.

Coming close, Heart saw the mare's coat was rough, mud-speckled. She was thin, too, her ribs jutting out.

Her tail was full of river burrs.

"Easy, now," Heart said softly. The mare lifted her head and turned. Heart could see scars on her face. The biggest one crossed her forehead, a curved band of stretched, dark skin.

"How did you survive that wound?" Heart whispered.

The mare lowered her head and came forward. Heart could smell her grass-sweet breath. The horse brushed Heart's cheek with her warm muzzle. Heart closed her eyes at the gentle touch.

"Catch it!" Simon shouted. "Use your belt!"

Heart opened her eyes and did as she was told. She untied her rough rope belt. The mare stood quietly. Then she lowered her head and let Heart slip the loop over her ears.

"Good girl!" Simon shouted. Heart glanced back. He was flapping his arms at her. He looked like a crow.

Heart tugged gently at the rope. The mare stepped forward, limping. Heart saw dark, dried blood on her foreleg.

"You're hurt," Heart said.

The mare touched Heart's cheek once more. Then she lowered her head. Heart held the rope loosely, careful not to walk too fast.

"Hurry along!" Simon shouted.

Heart pretended not to hear him. This mare needed rest and good forage. She needed care.

"Well, well," Simon said, rubbing his hands together.

As Heart got closer, she saw his eager expression fade.

"It's all scarred up," he growled. "And bone thin. Best to sell it to the knacker—before it dies. They pay less for dead."

Heart swallowed hard.

The knacker killed old animals and boiled the

meat for tallow. Candle makers and soap makers bought barrels of the smelly fat.

Heart shivered. "She's just hurt and starved."

Simon puffed out his cheeks. He was thinking it over. Heart held her breath. The mare stood behind her, still as stone.

"Bring it along then," Simon said.

The mare nudged Heart gently from behind. They followed Simon out of the field and up the slope to the road.

✦ CHAPTER TWO

Simon kept glancing back, motioning for Heart to catch up.

But the mare's limp was worse now that they were headed up the long hill on River Road.

Simon frowned over his shoulder. "Come on now, girl, come on!"

"I'm trying," Heart answered. "I'm tired, Simon."

She didn't want him to notice how lame the mare really was. He'd decide to go by the knacker's tonight after all. She could smell the stink of the tallow works as they passed Crosswater Street.

"Hurry," Simon kept insisting.

"I am," Heart said, without changing pace. But, as if she could understand human speech,

the mare limped along a little faster. Her clopping hooves scuffed up puffs of late-summer
dust.

It was good they had worked so late, Heart
thought. No one else was on the road.

Simon glanced back. "You are sure it isn't
Blackaby's horse?"

"Tin Blackaby owns no white horse," Heart
replied.

"You're certain?" Simon demanded.

"Yes," Heart said clearly. "I like horses. I
always stop and—"

"Good, then," Simon interrupted. "Lord
Dunraven would not own or want this wreck of
an animal—nor would any merchant. She's
some Gypsy's runaway." He smiled. "Luck has
smiled upon me."

Heart felt her belly tighten. "It has?"

Simon looked astonished. "Of course. I can
sell this old mare to the knacker now. Or maybe
later, after you feed her up a bit. I can make a
bit of silver."

Heart felt the mare's breath on the back of her neck. "I want to keep her."

"Keep the horse?" Simon slowed, frowning. "We can't feed it. Nobles, rich merchants, and Gypsies have horses, not people like us."

Heart walked after Simon in silence. The mare struggled to keep the pace he set. They crossed the broad arch of the bluff, then started downward again, passing Dunraven's orchards. There were fallen apples just inside the fence.

Heart spotted one that had rolled into the road.

The mare ate it whole, without slowing, tickling Heart's palm when she took it.

"I'll get up early to cut grass," Heart said. "She'll get sound and strong."

Simon turned. "She might get fatter. The knacker wants them fat."

Heart risked a quick smile.

Simon hadn't said no. There was hope. And once the mare was well, Heart would try to find work for them both, hauling or plowing. If the

mare brought in money, Simon would keep her.

Heart touched the mare's scarred face. "Meadowsweet will help your leg, I think. Ruth Oakes will know what to do."

The mare lifted her head.

They went south along River Road, skirting along the edge of town. By the time they turned onto Crooked Lane, heading toward Simon's shack, the mare's limp was terrible.

There were only two places on Crooked Lane. Ruth Oakes's old stone house stood near the turnoff, neat and well kept.

Simon's shack was two miles off, at the lane's end where the land dropped down to the river.

Heart tried to keep it neat. Simon did not help.

Heart saw Ruth Oakes's lantern as they passed. "I should go see about the mare's leg," she said.

Simon looked back. "In the morning."

"But the mare—" Heart began.

"In the morning," Simon repeated. "And tell

that old woman I can't pay." Simon's voice was heavy as stone.

They walked on in silence.

Finally, Simon cleared his throat.

"You can put it in the old cow pen if you prop up the broken rails." He coughed, then spat. "I'm hungry. And I suppose that means fixing my own supper tonight."

Heart didn't answer. She let the mare set her own, halting pace.

Simon went ahead.

There was lantern light shining through the door planks when Heart finally passed the shack, leading the mare toward the old cow pen.

Simon was eating supper.

Heart's mouth watered at the smell of boiled barley. But she knew she had another hour's work before she could eat.

It would take at least that long to make the sagging fence fit to hold a horse. Even if the horse was starved and hurt and weary.

✦ CHAPTER THREE

Heart was used to getting up in the dark. She always struck a spark and made a little fire for Simon's barley water.

This morning she started the fire, then tiptoed outside.

The moon sailed silent overhead. The river's quiet voice came up the grassy hill.

Heart peered into the dusk toward the makeshift corral. The mare was lying down. Her white coat shone in the moonlight.

Heart's bare feet made almost no sound in the deep dust of Crooked Lane. She ran uphill, grateful to see the bright speck of Ruth Oakes's lantern shining through her window.

Ruth stayed up late.

She also rose early.

She was Ash Grove's only healer. There was always so much for her to do.

Heart hurried up the curving path, the scents of Ruth's herb gardens tickling at her nose.

Heart could see Ruth through the window and knocked quietly.

"Yes?" Ruth called. "Come in!"

Heart pushed on the door. The light from the lantern made her blink.

"Child!" Ruth said. "And why are you at my door so early?"

Heart explained about the mare.

Ruth tipped her head and listened.

"A scarred forehead?" she asked, when Heart was finished.

Heart sighed. "Yes, but that's all healed. It's the wound on her leg that worries me."

"Let's go see," Ruth said, slinging her worn leather herb bag over her shoulder. She picked up her lantern, then headed for the door.

"Simon won't pay anything."

Ruth looked back, smiling. "And when did he ever pay me?"

Heart shrugged, uneasy. "I'll do chores. I'll work and—"

"And when did you ever *not* pay me in some way?" Ruth asked, starting off, quickly settling into her long-striding walk.

Heart ran to catch up.

The mare was standing when Ruth ducked through the fence.

"Oh, my," she said quietly.

"Is it that bad?" Heart whispered.

Ruth didn't answer. She placed one hand on the mare's withers and spoke to her in a quiet, soothing, singsong voice.

"Hold the lantern," she said after a moment.

Heart held the light steady and high, wincing when she saw the wound on the mare's leg clearly. It was deeper than she had thought.

"Fresh water," Ruth said, straightening. "We'll wash the road dust out of it, then seal it with meadowsweet salve."

Heart ran for the well.

The bucket was heavy, but Ruth took it in one

hand and tipped it to pour water slowly over the wound. Twice she stopped to dab at the cut with clean cloths from her bag.

The mare stood still, her head high.

"Will it heal?" Heart asked, biting at her lip.

Ruth nodded. "Yes. Another scar, but the lameness is just that it hurts her. The tendons aren't cut."

Heart exhaled. "I want to keep her. Simon wants to sell her to the knacker but—"

Ruth straightened and turned abruptly. "You can't let him."

Heart nodded. "I know. I love her already. She is the sweetest mare—"

Heart's words were cut off at the sound of the door banging open.

"Girl!"

"Her name is Heart Avamir," Ruth called out. "Not *Girl*."

"Did she tell you I won't pay a penny?" Simon groused.

Ruth laughed. "She did. The shock of it nearly killed me, Simon."

He growled something and went back inside.

"I'd better go cut grass for the mare," Heart said, looking at the horizon. "Sunup is coming and we have another field to glean today."

Ruth reached out suddenly and touched Heart's face. "You are a good-hearted child."

Heart smiled, wishing, as she had a thousand times, that Ruth had been the one to find her in the river grass instead of Simon.

Owing her life to Old Simon was a misery.

Owing Ruth Oakes would have been a joy.

Ruth stepped back. "Starting tomorrow, walk her just a little. Go a bit farther each day. It'll make her eat, and keep her leg from stiffening."

"I will," Heart promised.

Ruth handed her the pot of salve. "Twice a day, nice and thick."

Heart nodded, glancing at the door. "I had better go cut grass."

Ruth patted her arm. "Don't let that old man work you so hard."

✦ CHAPTER FOUR

No one in Ash Grove noticed the white mare.

Heart was careful.

She cut grass before dawn, hidden by the mists that rose from the Blue River.

She walked the mare only at dusk and always led her south, away from town.

To the south, the land was too dry and rocky to plow. No one farmed it. No one lived there.

People often came to Ruth Oakes's house, seeking her help. But no one walked two extra miles down to the end of Crooked Lane.

Adults had no business with Simon. He shouted and threw rocks at children who came too close—so they almost never did.

"Ready?" Heart said to the mare every evening.

And every evening, the mare tossed her mane and whickered quietly.

Ruth had given Heart a soft rope of woven flax.

Heart had made it into a knotted halter. The mare didn't like it, Heart could tell. But she allowed it.

Day by day the mare's limp faded. The cut closed and was healing well.

The heavy bundles of grass Heart brought were working magic. The mare gained weight. Her flesh smoothed over the bony ridges of her ribs. She stood with her head held high.

Heart found apples that had rolled beyond the fences around Lord Dunraven's orchards.

All the village children hunted these apples. Heart went before first light. Twice she had to run from boys who wanted to steal the ones she'd found. Both times, they had given up before the turnoff onto Crooked Lane. None of them wanted to be seen by Ruth Oakes—or to cross Old Simon's path.

"The horse is looking grand," Simon said one evening.

His voice startled Heart into whirling around. "I didn't hear you coming."

Simon nodded. "You were too busy talking to the mare." He shook his head, laughing, then ran one hand through his stubbly gray hair. "We can sell her soon. You've got her fat enough for any knacker."

"In another month or two, you could sell her as a saddle horse," Heart said quickly.

Simon stroked his chin with one hand. "Is she still limping?"

"A little," Heart fibbed. The mare hadn't limped for more than two weeks.

"You think she's strong enough to bear a rider?" Simon asked.

"Not yet," Heart said, pretending to consider the question. "But soon, I think."

"But that scar ruins her looks," Simon said, shaking his head. "What gentleman would want such an ugly saddle mare?"

Heart frowned at him. "She isn't ugly!"

"Lower your voice," Simon scolded.

Heart looked at her feet. Making Simon angry was foolish. "I'm sorry," she said.

Simon puffed out his cheeks. "Well, then. Keep feeding it," he said, jabbing one finger at the mare. "If no one else wants it, the knacker will."

"I thought maybe . . ." Heart began, then stopped.

"Thought what?" Simon asked.

"Maybe I could find an old plow. We could find work."

"We?" Simon repeated. "You mean you and the horse?"

Heart nodded.

Simon laughed. Then he spat. "Plowmen are *men*," he scoffed.

Heart stood tall. "I could plow."

Simon laughed. "You couldn't. It takes weight and strength."

Heart felt the mare tug her sleeve, nibbling at

the ragged cloth. Heart glanced at the sky. The sun was setting. "I need to take her out to walk."

"That where you go every evening after supper?"

Heart nodded. "Ruth Oakes said I should."

"That old faker," Simon said. "Her herbs aren't worth a half-penny." He headed back toward the house.

Heart waited until she heard the door slam.

Then she let out a long sigh.

"I will think of something," she told the mare, turning back. "Maybe we can get ahold of an old cart somehow. Would you pull a cart?"

The mare shook her mane.

Heart smiled; she loved it when the mare seemed to understand her. "We could carry messages. They say there's a man in Derrytown who carries letters for the merchants and nobles there."

The mare shook her mane again, snorting.

Heart frowned. "If we can earn a few pennies,

Simon will let me keep you." The mare lifted her head and flared her nostrils.

Heart pulled the halter down from its peg. The mare lowered her head as Heart slid it over her ears.

They passed Ruth Oakes's place and turned south as always. Out on River Road, the mare kept a good pace. As usual, she walked alongside Heart, not behind her.

The road was quiet. The air smelled of clean, fresh sage. The sounds and smells of town did not carry this far.

Heart glanced at the mare. She had never seen anyone but Dunraven's men or nobles like Tin Blackaby riding—and then only from a distance. She wanted to learn how.

Abruptly, the mare leapt sideways, wrenching hard at the halter.

Heart wasn't expecting it.

She lost her grip as the mare sprang into a canter.

Heart stood, stunned, as the mare galloped

away. Then she lunged after the horse, knowing it was useless. Aching inside, her eyes filling with tears, Heart ran on and on down the dusky road. The mare was a blurred speck of white in the dusk.

Finally, when Heart could run no more, she stumbled to a stop.

She bent over, gasping for breath.

In the distance, the muffled clatter of hooves had faded into silence.

The mare was gone.

Heart felt sick.

How could she have been so careless?

She trembled, still dragging in long breaths. Someone else would find the mare. Or wolves would.

Heart looked back toward Simon's shack. In the deepening dusk, it looked smaller and sadder than ever.

Heart stared at it.

Simon would be furious.

Ruth Oakes would be disappointed in her.

But that wasn't what hurt.

Now there'd be no reason to wake up excited. She would no longer have to get up early to cut grass and hunt extra apples—or hurry home.

A loneliness as sharp as thorns grew inside Heart. It filled her and she closed her eyes.

She was startled by a sudden cadence of distant hoofbeats. She caught her breath and opened her eyes, staring into the murky dusk.

Finally, she saw a blur of white.

The mare was galloping back toward her.

Astonished, Heart set her feet wide, ready to lunge for the halter.

But there was no need.

The mare dropped back to a canter, then a trot. She kept coming, her neck arched, breathing hard from the long gallop.

Heart felt joy rising inside her.

The mare looked grand indeed, trotting closer. She was stout now, her sides filled in, even swollen.

Heart narrowed her eyes.

There was something heavy in the mare's gait. Not the limp. That was gone. This was something different.

The mare stopped, standing so close that Heart simply lifted one hand to take hold of the halter.

The dusk around them had deepened. They stood in near darkness, so close Heart felt the warmth from the mare's run seeping into the chilly air. The mare pushed her muzzle into Heart's chest, blowing out deep breaths.

Keeping hold of the halter, Heart slid one hand over the mare's side. The tiniest flutter of movement beneath the white coat made Heart step back, blinking.

"You're in foal?" she breathed.

The mare shook her mane and stared off to the west. The sky was pink and orange now, the clouds colored like fire.

Heart pressed her palm against the white flank. The movement didn't return, but the fullness was unmistakable. Heart smiled.

The mare was going to have a baby.

Simon couldn't sell her now, not to the knacker or anyone else.

He *wouldn't*.

All he had to do was wait.

Two horses would be worth much more than one.

Heart put her arms around the mare's neck and began to cry.

✦ CHAPTER FIVE

Ruth Oakes knocked at the door early one morning. "I need to hire Heart," she told Simon. "I can't manage all my work."

"After she feeds the mare."

Heart stood up from her winnowing baskets and came to the door. "I cut grass before dawn, like always, Simon."

He turned away.

Halfway up Crooked Lane, Heart told Ruth the news. Ruth stopped, her hands on her hips. "Have you told Simon?"

Heart nodded.

"And his reaction?"

"He's whistling and humming over it." Heart scuffed her bare feet, making long marks in the dust.

They walked onward. "A foal," Ruth said softly. "Lovely. Any birth is like magic."

Heart smiled. "Her belly is getting bigger. She's eating as much as I can bring her."

"What have you named the mare?"

Heart glanced at Ruth. "I haven't. I don't know a name to give her."

"You could give her part of yours," Ruth said.

Heart liked the idea. Then the mare would be connected to her forever, like family. "Avamir?"

"It's a lovely name," Ruth agreed. "And an ancient one. That's why I chose it for you."

"Avamir, then," Heart agreed. She wanted to run back and tell the mare. But that was silly, of course. Horses didn't care about names.

Someone had left a box of fresh beets at Ruth's door.

Most of her patients paid her in trade.

She swung the box up and carried it inside. "Let's bundle the dried borage and hyssop, then we'll walk to market, if you're willing."

Heart smiled. "Of course."

Walking to town with Ruth meant no one would taunt her.

Every family in Ash Grove owed Ruth Oakes. Many of them loved her. No one wanted to offend her. Who could know when they would need the healer to come at midnight?

"These?" Heart asked, pointing at the drying racks.

Ruth nodded. "And the borage on the other side. I'll make packets of lobelia and verlane and . . ." She looked around the room. "Lemongrass, I think."

Heart fetched the cloth bags from the bin in the sunny kitchen.

She laid them out, then set to work. She was careful not to let too many crisp leaves scatter onto the floor.

"You do that better than I do now," Ruth said.

Heart grinned.

She loved being in this house.

"We'll use the peachwood baskets," Ruth said.

Heart ran to the storage room. The big peachwood baskets were reddish with arched handles.

"Perfect," Ruth said. "And a lovely day for the walk."

They followed River Road north, then turned on Crosswater Street.

The cobblestones were uneven.

Heart walked carefully—she didn't want to stub her bare toes.

After a few minutes, they crossed the creaking planks of the Tirin Creek Bridge and went on downhill.

"Look," Ruth said, pointing.

A mile ahead, coming across the long and narrow Blue River Bridge, carts and wagons turned toward Market Square. Derrytown merchants were arriving.

Ruth sighed. "A lot of them this morning. Maybe I should have brought more herbs."

"I would like to see Derrytown one day," Heart said aloud. "Maybe even Dunraven's castle."

Ruth patted her shoulder. "Then you shall."

It was not the answer Heart had expected. She laughed aloud.

"Good morning, Healer," someone called from across the street.

Heart saw Mrs. Renner; her husband ran the tallow works.

People moved away from Mrs. Renner as she walked. Tallow stink always clung to her clothes and hair. She had one son. Tibbs Renner was teased almost as much as Heart. She felt sorry for him, but she was afraid of him, too.

Ruth crossed the street to say hello to Mrs. Renner.

Heart waited, standing aside to let others go past.

"Psst. River foundling!"

Heart had been expecting this. Tibbs Renner was the biggest ten-year-old in Ash Grove. And the meanest.

Heart tensed as he walked up.

"I saw you with that horse," he said. "Where'd you steal it?"

Heart's breath caught. She had hoped no one had seen Avamir. "I found her. In the woods," she told him.

"Found her?" Tibbs sneered. "No one ever just *finds* a horse."

"I did," Heart said as evenly as she could.

"Liar," he said. "Why are you hiding the horse then?"

Heart blinked. "I'm not, really. I just thought people might—"

"Spread the word about it? Find the real owner?" Tibbs interrupted.

Looking past him, Heart saw Ruth saying good-bye to his mother.

"She was loose in the woods, no bridle or saddle and she was hurt terribly and—"

"Liar," Tibbs said. "That's one thing the healer can't cure—lying."

"Heart needs no such cure," Ruth said from behind him.

Tibbs jumped. "I was joking," he said quickly.

Ruth looked at him sternly. "I would hate to think you were insulting my friend."

Tibbs mumbled something and walked away. But he glanced back, flushed and scowling.

Ruth sighed. Then she led off, turning down Trader's Path when they came to it.

Trader's Path was the oldest—and the shortest and narrowest—street in Ash Grove. It veered toward the river, then back to run along the edge of Market Square. People on foot used it. The wagons went around to Market Street.

Heart loved the smells and colors of the Market Square.

She wished they could stay all day.

But they never did.

The booths were setting up.

Ruth walked fast, going up and down the aisles, saying hello to nearly everyone they passed. She stopped at a few booths.

The herbs sold quickly.

Ruth's medicines were known to be pure and strong.

Walking home, Heart saw Tibbs coming toward them. He gave a quick nod, and hurried past.

"That boy makes me worry," Ruth said.

Heart's stomach knotted up.

It didn't loosen until she ran the length of Crooked Lane and saw the mare standing safe in her fence.

Heart hugged her neck, clinging hard.

"Avamir?" she said when she stepped back. "Do you like that name?"

The mare shook her mane and rubbed her broad cheek against Heart's shoulder.

"Was there a boy out here today?" Heart asked.

Avamir shook her mane and stamped a fore hoof.

Then she went back to picking at scattered blades of grass in the apple crate that served as her hay rick.

✦ CHAPTER SIX

Heart worked for Ruth every chance she got.

At first, Simon complained about cleaning barley by himself.

Then, in October, he groused about digging potatoes without her.

He was upset having to make his own supper in December and January. By February, Heart finally reminded him loudly of all the pennies she was earning.

He frowned. And he kept complaining.

"Are you feeding that mare well enough?" he asked at least once a week.

"Of course," Heart said evenly, every time he asked.

Heart was happier than she had ever been.

Tibbs still stared at her. But he left her alone.

And every evening when she walked Avamir, she let go of the halter as soon as they were far from town.

Avamir loved to gallop, free as wind.

Heart loved to watch her.

The galloping had slowed somewhat, of course.

Avamir was very heavy now, her belly full with her growing foal.

Heart felt it moving nearly every time she pressed her palms on Avamir's flank.

Ruth said that meant the foal was close. She said she would come to help if Avamir needed her.

"When will she drop that foal?" Simon asked every single evening in March.

Heart just shrugged.

She didn't know. She couldn't know. When Ruth needed to go to the market, Heart was impatient to get back.

"Give me the pennies," Simon said every time she got home from Ruth's house.

Heart handed them to him.

Then he would ask his second question.

"Is that all?"

Heart had never hidden or kept back even one penny. The question insulted her.

"Would it be wrong to keep a few pennies?" Heart asked Ruth one fair morning in May.

The healer stopped her work and turned. "Doesn't he let you?"

Heart shook her head. "Never. Nary a one."

Ruth frowned. She looked out the window toward Simon's shack. "Keep half. But be honest. Tell him. Then hide them well."

"Half?" Heart breathed. "Is that fair?"

"Half." Ruth said it flatly. "More than fair," she added. "He's gotten dawn to dusk work out of you since he found you." She reached up and took down a wooden box. "Here. Bury it outside somewhere safe."

"I wish I had parents," Heart heard herself saying. Then she blushed.

"You do have parents, of course," Ruth said softly. "It's a matter of finding them."

Heart looked down at her hands.

Flecks of red mallow leaves were stuck to her nails.

"Do you think I ever will?" she asked.

Ruth exhaled. "I do. Now help me with the valerian roots, will you? I have them soaking in the copper tub."

A few days later, Heart told Simon she was keeping half her pennies.

He roared, then whined.

Then he went silent for a few hours.

The next morning he acted as though the argument had never happened.

That night, after he was asleep, Heart buried the box beside the corral.

One evening, going home, Heart saw someone dodge between two trees on River Road, running back toward town.

The sun was low and glaring, but it looked like Tibbs Renner.

Heart's skin prickled.

What was he doing?

Heart ran all the way from Ruth's house to Simon's shack, and headed straight for Avamir's corral.

The mare whickered as Heart ducked between the crooked rails.

"Are you all right?" Heart asked her. "Was Tibbs here? Did he scare you?"

The mare nudged Heart, pushing her back gently. She seemed fine.

Heart felt herself calming down. "I'm a little late," she apologized to the mare. "We better go or it'll be too dark."

Heart slid the rails aside. But, for the first time, Avamir wasn't eager to get out.

"Did he hurt you?" Heart searched the mare's silky white coat for wounds or lumps from rock bruises. Tibbs was a great aim with a rock. He liked to show off.

Avamir turned away, then paced a tight circle, switching her tail.

Then she lay down, dropping heavily to her knees. She groaned quietly.

Heart caught her breath, scared, but beginning to understand. "Avamir? Is your baby coming?" she asked softly. "Are you ready to foal?"

Avamir didn't respond to the sound of her name as she usually did. Heart could tell she was listening intently to something else.

Something inside herself.

Heart ran for clean rags and was glad when she saw Simon asleep on his cot.

She tiptoed in, then out, carrying her own cot blanket along with the rags.

Avamir was groaning.

It was a deep sound unlike anything Heart had ever heard.

The mare strained, then relaxed, gulping in long breaths.

Stars came out overhead one by one. The moon rose and climbed in the sky, full and round.

Avamir strained over and over, until her white coat was soaked with sweat.

Heart stayed close, draping the blanket over the mare's back so she wouldn't get chilled.

"Should I get Ruth?" Heart asked the sky. "Does Avamir need help?"

Avamir shook her mane, then lifted her head and nudged at Heart's shoulder.

"Do you want me to stay?" Heart pleaded.

She was afraid to leave the mare alone.

She was just as afraid to wait any longer to run for help.

What if Avamir was having trouble?

Suddenly, Avamir groaned, her whole body trembling with effort.

Heart saw two tiny hooves emerge.

The next push brought spindly front legs and a muzzle small enough to drink from a teacup.

Heart held her breath.

Avamir made an odd sound, somewhere between pain and joy. She strained again.

The foal slid into the world and lay still on the ground.

Then it curled like a fish without air.

Heart frantically wiped away the birth water from its nostrils and eyes. She soaked one rag and picked up another.

The foal wriggled in her arms.

Avamir turned to lick at her baby.

Heart kept rubbing. Together they dried the foal and helped it stand on its own skinny legs. The foal's coat was purest white. In the moonlight, it looked silvery.

"Moonsilver," Heart whispered, and smiled.

It was the perfect name.

✦ CHAPTER SEVEN

The morning after the foal was born, Simon stood by the fence, frowning. "Look at it! It's ugly."

Heart stared at the baby horse that had slept in her arms. "He's only a little small. He'll grow and—"

"Small?" Simon exploded. "It's sickly like its mother!"

Heart shook her head, moving a step closer to Avamir. "She was half starved, Simon. And hurt. Not sickly."

He rubbed his chin. "What's wrong with its face?"

Heart bit her lip. The foal's head was oddly formed. It worried her. "Nothing," she said aloud.

"Its forehead is misshapen. It's swollen. Maybe it has brain fever?"

"No," Heart said.

"Tonight, you should walk them up the road for that old woman to take a look," Simon said.

Heart glanced at him. "I will."

"Tell her I won't pay her a penny."

Heart lifted her chin. "I will pay her."

Simon flashed her an angry look. "I suppose you can do what you like with *your* pennies."

"He isn't sickly," Heart said as Simon turned away.

But all day she was worried.

She did her work. She hoed their little garden and swept the house and cleaned the hearth.

She went to gather deadwood with Simon for their fire. Walking home with the heavy sacks, Heart walked as fast as Simon would go.

The worry knot in her stomach had been tightening all day. Passing Ruth's house, she peered inside. The old woman was there. Good.

Once the firewood was stacked, Simon sat in

his chair with a sigh. Heart ran for the horses. The dusk was thickening.

"Moonsilver isn't sick," Ruth told her. They stood outside her door, the lantern on the garden wall.

Heart let out a breath. "Are you sure?"

"I am," Ruth said, keeping her eye on Avamir.

The mare's ears were back. She kept circling to stand between Ruth and her foal.

"His forehead—"

"I see that," Ruth interrupted. "It is odd. But look at how quick he is. He seems very strong for a new foal."

Heart let out a long breath. Of course Ruth was right.

"Just feed Avamir every bit you can manage. The foal will grow strong and straight if her milk is rich."

"I will," Heart promised.

She kept her word.

Every day, she walked a mile down to the river and back to cut heavy bundles of tender grass.

She hunted by moonlight for fallen early plums along Lord Dunraven's fence.

She even saved boiled barley or wheat from her own suppers.

Avamir had plenty of milk.

Moonsilver nursed constantly.

But he stayed small and thin.

In the warm June evenings, Heart took the horses up to River Road. Avamir galloped as fast as ever. Moonsilver kept up with her. His legs were spindly, but he ran like lightning.

As summer nights warmed, Ruth's herbs needed setting. Then they needed weeding, and, finally, they had to be cut and dried. Heart learned that each plant was different.

Some loved damp soil, others rotted in it.

Some grew fast in bright sun, others died without shade.

Some days they gathered wild herbs.

Heart loved the long walks into the woods. Meadowsweet and velvety verbain, lobelia and prickly Colter's Wart . . . Heart learned where each herb hid in the forest.

And she was learning what they were used for.

On market days, Heart usually went to town with Ruth Oakes.

But it was different now.

Ruth started selling her herbs at one end of Market Square.

Heart began at the other.

They visited every customer's booth, selling everything they had brought and doing it twice as fast.

Heart often saw Tibbs Renner. He never spoke to her, but she caught him staring, sometimes. In a way, she was glad when she saw him. At least she knew he wasn't out poking around Simon's place, bothering Avamir.

Ruth always said hello to Tibbs—but then Ruth said hello to everyone.

"I saw Tibbs on River Road," Heart told Ruth on the way home after the first market day in July.

"Where?"

"Up by your place, headed back into town.

I was afraid he had done something to Avamir."

Ruth looked sad as they walked on. Her silence lasted a long time.

Finally, she straightened her apron, jingling the day's coins.

"Tibbs is mean because his father is mean to him. And the children taunt him."

"They taunt me, too," Heart said.

"Yes, but his father . . ." Ruth began, then fell silent again.

Heart wondered if her own father had been kind or cruel.

She tried, for the thousandth time, to follow her memories backward. They stopped where they always had. Before that day in the river grass, she had no memories at all.

"I do wish Simon hadn't sold the blanket," she said quietly.

Ruth sighed, understanding her. "It was lovely. Silver thread embroidery of unicorns."

"Unicorns," Heart echoed. Simon had not told her that.

Ruth smiled. "I saw it. Old fashioned, by a hundred years. No one believes any of those old stories now."

"My parents must be rich, then," Heart said. "If they owned a fine old blanket like that. So why would they just leave me?"

"I don't know." Ruth reached out to touch Heart's cheek. "But you will find out one day, I am sure."

Heart was unable to think of anything to say. She pulled in a deep breath. "Tibbs stares at me. He hates me, I think."

"We'll both watch for Tibbs," Ruth said, turned down Crooked Lane and headed for her house. "If he causes trouble, I'll help." She opened her front door and went inside. "Just leave Tin Blackaby out of it. The boy has enough trouble."

Heart followed Ruth into the kitchen, thinking.

If children stole or set fires, or did other terrible things, Tin Blackaby could arrest them. There were prisons in Dunraven's castle.

Heart could recall three boys being sent away.

None had ever come back.

"I won't tell Tin Blackaby anything," she promised.

"Thank you," Ruth said. "If Tibbs gets his chance, he'll turn out all right."

Ruth found her lantern and lit it, then spilled the day's money out onto her kitchen table. Heart added the coins she had collected.

Ruth made two stacks. One was a little smaller. She pushed it toward Heart.

"You've learned a great deal these past months," she said. "We can be partners now."

Heart was astonished. "I haven't learned nearly enough."

Ruth smiled. "I agree. But you will."

Heart stared at the money.

If Ruth made her partner, she might someday have enough to buy *shoes*. And she would save every penny after that so maybe she really could see Derrytown and Dunraven's castle one day.

Heart imagined herself riding Avamir into Derrytown. Moonsilver would run along loose behind them, strong and beautiful, his hooves dancing on the road.

She would wear a new red coat and soft leather boots.

People would wonder who she was.

"Take it," Ruth said. "You have earned it."

Heart stared at the coins, then swept them up and put them into her pockets.

"Thank you." The words seemed far too small so she said them again.

"Thank you."

Heart's partnership with Ruth meant she was gone all day every day.

She gave Simon some of her money, so he didn't scold her. As August passed and September came, he began gleaning the fields. The harvesters had been too quick again. They had been careless. The fields were full of missed grain.

Simon came home with a heavy sack every evening, smiling.

Then one evening, Simon met Heart at the

door. He was frowning, but said nothing until supper. "Tin Blackaby has called a meeting," he told her then. "One of his men pounded at the door today to tell me."

Heart looked up from her bowl of boiled wheat.

"No one knows what it's about," Simon said in a low voice. "Can't be anything good. His meetings never are."

Heart nodded, her stomach tightening. "When?"

"Tomorrow evening. You'll have to skip the mare's gallop."

Heart nodded and stood, her appetite gone.

Simon saw the barley in her dish and reached to pick it up. "That fool mare and colt," he muttered.

Heart didn't answer, but she knew what he was thinking.

He was afraid something they had done was the cause of the trouble.

Everyone in Ash Grove would be afraid of the same thing tonight.

✦ CHAPTER EIGHT

River Road was as full of people as Heart had ever seen it. Everyone was walking slowly, quietly. Simon was silent, frowning.

Where River Road met Crosswater Street, they turned toward Market Square with all the rest.

"There are hundreds coming," Simon muttered as they slowed with the thickening crowd. "Even the old ones and babies. Blackaby must have sent messengers to every door."

Heart looked around as they walked.

Simon was right.

There were people so old that their grandchildren had to help them walk.

She saw Tibbs just as they turned onto Trader's Path.

He was with his family.

Mr. Renner looked angry.

Heart saw Mr. Renner shove at Tibbs, saying something close to his ear. Tibbs looked scared.

"Stop staring at them," Simon said, tugging at Heart's sleeve. "I want no arguments with the knacker."

Tin Blackaby had had his men build a platform at one end of Market Square.

He stood upon it, his mouth a thin, angry line.

In front of the platform, a row of his men faced the crowd, their arms crossed.

The back of the square filled up first.

No one wanted to stand near Blackaby's men.

Heart and Simon ended up in the middle. People stood close together, but no one spoke.

Tin Blackaby stared at them until people began to clear their throats and glance around uneasily.

"The harvesters this year were careless," he shouted, finally, startling everyone. Heart felt her pulse quicken.

"No one bothered to tell me this," he accused them. "No one told me, so I could not tell Lord Dunraven."

Heart noticed a tall figure in a black cloak standing behind Tin Blackaby.

Had the man been there all along?

"I could not tell our lord that he had been cheated." Tin Blackaby's voice was rough and loud.

Heart noticed people drawing even closer together.

Everyone looked straight ahead.

"How many of you noticed that the fields had been harvested poorly these past two seasons?"

Heart waited.

No one put up a hand.

No one called out.

Tin Blackaby muttered something Heart couldn't hear, then he raised his voice again. "You have all shamed me before Lord Dunraven," he said. "I told him you were honest.

I said you would admit a mistake. But I see I was wrong."

The tall figure stepped forward suddenly and Tin Blackaby dropped to one knee. He bowed his head.

The man in the black cloak pushed back his hood.

Heart had never seen Lord Dunraven, but she knew that's who he was.

He had long silver hair. Even from where Heart stood she could tell that he had narrow, angry eyes. And when he spoke, his voice was like thunder.

"People of Ash Grove. Be grateful that I am honest and fair. Be glad I will not punish you."

The crowd stirred as people exchanged nervous glances. No one spoke.

"Tomorrow at dawn, men will come to your homes. They will collect my share of the wheat and barley you have gleaned from my fields: Half."

Lord Dunraven paused nearly a full minute

before he spoke again. "And if you ever cheat me again, I'll make you sorry."

He waited another full minute, then he gestured like a farmer shooing away pesky dogs. "Go home."

Heart followed Simon out of the square.

No one was talking.

Even the smallest children were quiet.

Heart scanned the crowd.

Where was Ruth Oakes? Maybe she was tending someone too sick to leave?

"It isn't fair," someone said clearly.

"Shhh!" an old man hissed.

"He's right though," someone else muttered.

No one responded.

They trudged back up the hill to River Road. The sun set and dusk darkened the sky. By the time they got to Crooked Lane, it was nearly dark. Only then did Simon speak.

"Get a halter on that mare."

Heart was startled. "Why?"

"As soon as it's pitch dark, you're taking

her to the knacker's. Her and the colt."

Heart shook her head. "Why? No one said anything about them."

"Maybe Blackaby's man didn't notice them. But Dunraven's man will." Simon made a chopping motion with one hand. "If they go to the knacker's tonight, I get paid. And there's no trouble with Dunraven's man come morning."

"No!" Heart breathed. "You can't ask me to do that."

"Why not?" Simon demanded. "I will do it if you won't. That colt isn't worth raising. I'll give you some of the money, of course," he added, softening his voice.

Heart wanted to scream at him.

She held it back.

She bit her lip.

And she nodded. "I'll take them, then."

"Good girl," Simon said. Then he went inside, slamming the door behind him.

✦ CHAPTER NINE

Heart put the halter on Avamir.

She told Simon she was cold and carried her ragged coat and her blanket outside.

She waited five minutes.

Then she went back in.

"I need some rags," she told Simon calmly. "I want to braid a halter for the colt, too. He might run off."

"That's my girl," Simon said proudly. "Thinking and planning." He was sitting by the fire.

He yawned. The long walk to town on top of the day's work had worn him out.

Heart hummed softly as she made a braided halter for the colt. She saw Simon yawn again.

Still humming, Heart took two of the four

apples on the sideboard. She filled a sack with cleaned barley. She took a striking flint and steel to make a fire. She packed the smallest cook pot. She took twine, bobbins, and a needle and everything else she could think of that Simon owned and could spare.

Then she went outside and dug up the little box that held her money. She left a stack of copper pennies on Simon's table to pay for what she was taking, then went outside again.

Shivering in the evening chill, Heart haltered Avamir. She put the braided halter on the colt, but let him run free behind as she started off, walking slowly.

She half-expected Simon to hear the hoof beats and come running out the door.

He didn't.

She thought Ruth might come out to ask where she was going.

But that didn't happen, either.

Ruth's windows were dark. She was probably at someone's house, nursing a sick person.

Heart blinked back tears.

Ruth's advice—a warm hug—Heart wanted both more than anything else in the world. But she was on her own and she knew it. She wasn't even going to get to say good-bye.

Heart tried to think clearly.

She and the horses would starve on the empty plains in winter. Open wheat and barley fields were useless to her.

The forests and mountains across the Blue River were her only hope of hiding.

Heart walked the mare toward town, trembling and afraid. Moonsilver came behind, staying close to his mother.

River Road was dark.

Crosswater Street was empty.

After she crossed the Tirin Creek Bridge, Heart could hear men's voices in Market Square. If they heard Avamir's hooves clopping they paid no attention.

She glanced eastward and saw a glow on the horizon.

The moon was rising.

Halfway across the bridge over the Blue River, the moon came up. Heart kept walking, clenching her teeth.

Then suddenly, shouts broke out behind her. Heart began to run, pulling at the halter.

Avamir balked, jerking Heart to a halt.

"Come on!" Heart whispered, dragging at the flaxen rope. The voices were getting louder. "I think they saw us," Heart pleaded, her pulse pounding in her temples. If they were caught now, with Tin Blackaby already so angry . . .

Avamir shook her mane.

Then she bent one knee and sank down on the bridge planks, kneeling like a trick horse.

For a long second, Heart thought the mare was hurt.

Then she understood.

Heart swung one leg awkwardly over Avamir's back.

The mare straightened.

Heart nearly fell, grasping at Avamir's mane

as the mare trotted, then cantered, her hoof-beats thunderous in the silent night. Moonsilver galloped after his mother, his own hoofbeats a rain-patter on the bridge planks.

Heart could not sit upright.

She had never ridden a horse in her life.

The quick rhythm of the mare's gait terrified her.

Heart closed her eyes and tangled her fingers in Avamir's mane, bouncing awkwardly on the mare's back as the voices faded behind them.

After a long time, Avamir slowed, breathing hard. Then she stopped and stood still.

Heart opened her eyes. Slowly, she released her grip on the mare's mane. Her hands were cramped.

Swinging down to the ground. Heart faced Avamir.

"You are the smartest horse I ever heard of," Heart said.

Avamir lifted her head and began to walk.

Moonsilver trotted after her.

Heart ran to catch up, grabbing at Avamir's halter. Side by side they walked deeper into the forest.

They walked until the moon was high overhead.

Then Heart stopped.

Her legs trembling from weariness and fear, Heart found a dense stand of trees—a safe place to build a tiny fire.

Too nervous to sleep, she sat still as Avamir and the colt settled onto beds of pine needles close by.

Heart ringed the fire with rocks and warmed a little barley in her cook pot.

She heard wolves howling far away and shivered.

Staring into the flames as the horses dozed, she tried to figure out what to do.

She could just keep going and try to live in the deep woods. Or she could try to find a village where she might manage to earn a living.

But Heart knew everyone she met would think she'd stolen the horses.

Girls dressed in raggedy clothes never owned horses, after all.

Heart looked at Avamir, her white coat shining in the firelight. Moonsilver slept beside her. An odd shadow darkened his odd, bulging forehead, making him even less pretty than usual.

Heart stood up, narrowing her eyes. Was the colt hurt?

Stepping around the fire, Heart knelt beside him. The shadow was a stain. Blood was seeping into his smooth white coat.

He must have cantered into a low branch, she decided, touching the wound. But it wasn't bad, no more than the skin broken.

Heart sighed in relief.

Then a strange glitter caught her attention.

She peered at Moonsilver's forehead.

There, peeking through the edges of the colt's broken skin, was a gleam of silver.

Holding her breath, Heart touched it carefully, knowing what it was, but not ready to believe it.

The hard, slick nub of a horn felt cold, like winter ice.

A unicorn's horn.

The awful scar on Avamir's face suddenly made sense.

So did her amazing intelligence.

"You're unicorns?" Heart whispered.

Avamir shook her mane and extended her muzzle. Heart felt the warm sweet breath on her cheek. Then Avamir lowered her head and closed her eyes to sleep.

Heart sat very still.

Unicorns?

Unicorns weren't real. They were legends, nothing more.

Heart tried to remember the tales she had heard. She was pretty sure people in the old stories were afraid of unicorns. She remembered something about people killing them for their magical horns.

Heart looked up at the sky.

Ruth had told her once that her blanket had had unicorns embroidered on it.

Heart shivered and moved closer to the fire.

Simon would sell her unicorns to Lord

Dunraven. So would Tibbs Renner if he got a chance. A lot of people would. And Dunraven might kill Moonsilver to cut off his horn.

Heart shuddered, feeling sick. This much was certain: Lord Dunraven would never let her see Avamir or Moonsilver again.

A breeze whispered through the treetops.

Heart stared into the flames of her campfire.

Maybe she could gather herbs and trade them for food at the Ash Grove Market, leaving Avamir and Moonsilver in the forest.

Ruth Oakes would help, if she could.

Heart took a deep breath and promised the starry sky that she would protect Avamir and Moonsilver.

She loved them both.

Whatever it cost—even her life—she would keep them safe.

· THE END ·